CAVERN CAPTIVES

A rabbit jumped out from behind some brush. The startled man raised his gun and fired. The rabbit fell to the ground.

Will looked through a crack in the brush. He was crouched down—waiting, hoping. He saw the rabbit fall. The big man walked within two feet of him. Will held his breath.

"All right, boy. Have it your way. But if you go for the cops, I'll kill her personally."

The man turned and walked away.

Will didn't dare come out for fear that Scarface might hear something and come back.

He waited there, hardly breathing for what seemed an eternity. His mind was blank except for one thought . . .

Sarah.

YEARLING BOOKS/YOUNG YEARLINGS/YEARLING CLASSICS are designed especially to entertain and enlighten young people. Patricia Reilly Giff, consultant to this series, received her bachelor's degree from Marymount College and a master's degree in history from St. John's University. She holds a Professional Diploma in Reading and a Doctorate of Humane Letters from Hofstra University. She was a teacher and reading consultant for many years, and is the author of numerous books for young readers.

For a complete listing of all Yearling titles,
write to
Dell Readers Service,
P.O. Box 1045,
South Holland, IL 60473.

THE LEGEND OF
RED HORSE
CAVERN

A YEARLING BOOK

Published by
Bantam Doubleday Dell Books for Young Readers
a division of
Bantam Doubleday Dell Publishing Group, Inc.
1540 Broadway
New York, New York 10036

ISBN: 0-440-41023-1

Series design: Barbara Berger

Printed in the United States of America

October 1994

10 9 8 7 6 5 4 3 2 1

OPM

Dear Readers:

Real adventure is many things—it's danger and daring and sometimes even a struggle for life or death. From competing in the Iditarod dogsled race across Alaska to sailing the Pacific Ocean, I've experienced some of this adventure myself. I try to capture this spirit in my stories, and each time I sit down to write, that challenge is a bit of an adventure in itself.

You're all a part of this adventure as well. Over the years I've had the privilege of talking with many of you in schools, and this book is the result of hearing firsthand what you want to read about most—power-packed action and excitement.

You asked for it—so hang on tight while we jump into another thrilling story in my World of Adventure.

Gary Paulsen

THE LEGEND OF RED HORSE CAVERN

CHAPTER 1

The moon cast eerie shadows as a velvet darkness covered the Sacramento Mountain range. The young brave sat quietly in the thicket and stared out across the meadow. An old doe raised her head and looked cautiously toward the brush where he was hiding. There was a time when he would have been interested in hunting her, but not tonight. Tonight he was on a quest.

A quest to help his people.

His hand touched the soft leather pouch hanging from his neck. The Old One had filled it with powerful medicine to help fight *the evil. His hand traveled to the quiver on his back, which contained five new arrows. He would need only two: one for the white prospector and one for Red Horse—the betrayer.*

A movement.

They were coming. He silently slipped one of the arrows from the quiver and fitted it to his bow. He could see their outlines clearly. He raised the bow, took careful aim, and . . .

"Will." A voice split the mountain air.

"William Little Bear Tucker. I am speaking to you."

Will blinked. He looked up into the face of his best friend, Sarah Thompson.

She glared at him. "Are we or are we not going to explore this cave today?"

"I was just—"

"I know exactly what you were doing. You were pretending you were the brave in that old legend again." She turned on her flashlight and stepped inside the cave. "Come back to reality and let's have a look around."

Will followed her. "All right. You don't have to get mad about it."

"I'm not mad. It's just that we've been planning on exploring this cave ever since we found the opening last week. My little brother saw me packing my backpack, and I had to give him my best comic to keep his mouth shut about it. My mom gets worried every time we come to Ghost Mountain."

"I'm sorry. I guess the reason I think about the legend so much is that my grandfather loves to tell it."

"I know. I've heard it so often I can almost repeat it word for word." She hopped up on a nearby boulder, put her hand over her heart, and lowered her voice to sound more like Will's grandfather.

"Once, many years ago, my people, the Apaches, lived in these mountains. There was plenty of game, and the fish never ran out. The times were happy. Then one year it forgot to rain. The streams dried up, and the game went away."

Will jumped in. "Kaetennae, the Old One, told the people it was because they had angered the rain god. To appease him, they must bring all their gold and jewelry to be melted into a statue in his honor.

"Then one day a prospector discovered the

golden statue and made plans to steal it. He was aided in this evil by Red Horse, a brave who had lived with the whites and despised the traditions of his people.

"Every man and boy in the tribe went after the two thieves. They finally found them in Rancho Rio Canyon, not far from here. But they didn't find what they expected.

"The white prospector was stretched out over an anthill—dead. The body of Red Horse lay a few feet away. But his head was missing. The braves looked and looked for the head but they never found it. The head, along with the gold statue, was never seen again."

Sarah made a spooky noise and wiggled her fingers. "And the headless ghost, the spirit of Red Horse, is still up here roaming the canyon, searching for his head. Because unless he finds it and does something to bring honor back upon himself, his spirit can never be free."

Sarah shuddered. "The whole thing gives me the creeps." She moved farther into the cave. "Boy, this place is bigger than I thought. I still don't see the back."

Will flashed his light around on the glistening walls. "It's huge. You could live in here. It's bigger than a house."

Sarah moved to the back of the cave. "Will, take a look at this."

He shifted the weight of his backpack. "What is it?"

"There's a passage back here. Let's see where it leads."

The passage was narrow at first but gradually opened into another larger room. Crystal-covered stalactites hung from the ceiling. Large brown stalagmites grew from the floor.

Will's teeth were chattering. "I didn't know it would be so cold in here."

Sarah pointed her light around the new room. There were passageways taking off in every direction. "This is so neat. It'll take us forever to explore all of these."

Will pointed the light at his watch. "We don't have a lot of time. I told Grandfather we'd be back in time for supper."

Sarah flipped her French braid behind her back. "We'll just try a couple. My mom told me the same thing. She heard some news report about an armored truck shipment being held up a few days ago, and she's convinced we'll all be killed in our sleep."

Will headed into the left passage. The walls glistened like shiny marble. "This is so incredible, Sarah. We're probably the first people ever to see the inside of this place."

The passage narrowed. The air was musty, and they had to duck to avoid the stalactites.

Will flashed his light around the tiny room. "Wouldn't it be great if the legend of the rain god were true and we found the golden statue down here?"

Sarah made a face. "The statue part would be all right. I'm not too sure about finding Red Horse's head though."

Sarah pointed her light at the far end of the cavern wall. "What was that?" Something gold reflected the light.

They both spoke at once. "The statue!"

Will jumped over a small boulder and ran for the shiny object. He tripped and fell to the rocks on one knee. A jagged stalagmite ripped his flesh. Pain tore through his body.

"Are you all right?" Sarah held the light on his leg. His pants were torn, and blood was trickling out of an open gash.

"It looks bad, Will. We'd better get you out of here."

Will shook his head. "Reach in my pack. I wrapped some apples with a bandanna. Get it for me."

She quickly pulled out the bandanna and handed it to him.

"Point your light over here." He folded the cloth and tied it around his leg the way his grandfather had taught him. "There. That ought to hold it for a while."

Sarah was still rummaging in his backpack. "Look at all this stuff. You've got everything from ropes to flares in here."

Will jerked it away from her. "I like to be prepared." He eased himself into a standing position. "Come on. Let's see what's over there."

"I don't know, Will. You're hurt pretty bad, and this place is spooky. Maybe we should come back another day."

"It'll only take a minute." Will made his

way to the edge of the wall. "Well, how about that? I guess we're not the first people to explore down here after all."

Sitting on a ledge in front of them, shimmering in the flashlight's soft glow, was an old-fashioned metal trunk.

Chapter 2

 "It's locked." Will sat down on the ledge beside the trunk. "What I wouldn't give for a hacksaw right about now."

Sarah sat down beside him. "You know what this means, don't you?"

"Yeah. If we can get this thing open, we'll be filthy rich."

"That's not what I'm talking about. Think about it. How did that chest get in here?"

Will shrugged. "Somebody hid it here."

"Don't you get it? There weren't any tracks the way we came. There has to be another entrance."

He hit his forehead with the palm of his hand. "Duh. Of course. I was so busy thinking about treasure I didn't stop to think about how the trunk got here. But now that you mention it, there is a lot of fresh air in here. It has to be coming from somewhere."

"Maybe tomorrow we can find the other entrance."

Will stood up on his good leg. "Why not now?"

"It was nearly dark when we came in here. Your grandfather will be worried if you don't show up pretty soon."

"I guess you're right." Will patted the chest. "This thing's not going anywhere. We'll come back and explore some more tomorrow."

Sarah put her backpack on one shoulder. She took the light. "I'll lead the way back to the entrance. If I go too fast for you, holler."

Sarah made one last sweep of the room with the light. "It looks like a palace." She held the light on a big rock. "There's the throne."

Will hobbled over to it and sat down. "How do I look? Would I make a good king?"

"I don't know. I was thinking it looked more like a throne for a queen."

Will picked up a handful of gravel and tossed it at her. "That'll be the day."

Sarah moved into the small passage where they'd started. "I can see daylight."

A deep voice boomed at her. "But not for long, sister."

Will swung around. Two burly men were holding guns on them.

CHAPTER 3

The shorter man had a mustache and wore a brown felt cowboy hat. The bigger one had a wide scar running from his cheek to his neck.

The short man spoke first. "Take them in the back to one of those bottomless holes we found. Push them over the edge. No one will be the wiser. Don't fire your gun unless you have to."

Will was stunned. These men were serious. They actually intended to kill them.

"You heard him." The man with the scar

pushed Will and motioned with his gun for them to go ahead of him.

Sarah bent over. "I just need to tie my shoe." She came up with two handfuls of thick black dirt and threw it in Scarface's eyes.

"Run, Will!"

Will didn't hesitate. His leg burned like fire from his wound, but he ran for all he was worth. When he reached the entrance he didn't slow down. He ran into the forest until he was sure no one was following him.

The short man grabbed Sarah by her braid. "That was stupid." He slapped her hard across the face and knocked her to the ground.

Shorty yelled at Scarface. "Go after him, you idiot. Let him know that if he goes for the cops, we'll kill the girl."

Scarface glared at Sarah. "I owe you one, girlie. I'll be back."

Shorty growled after him, "Don't come back without that kid."

The big man stumbled down the passage

and out the cave's entrance. The bright sunlight blinded him. He searched the ground for Will's footprints and started tracking him.

"Come here, sonny. Let's talk. Listen, I wasn't really going to hurt you. Shorty just said that to scare you."

The big man still had his gun out. He followed Will to a cluster of pine trees and then lost his trail in the pine needles. He wiped his brow with a dirty handkerchief.

"Come on out, boy. I'm through playing games. We have your girlfriend. She's not going to look so pretty after a while. If you come out, I'll let you both go."

A rabbit jumped out from behind some brush. The startled man raised his gun and fired. The rabbit fell to the ground.

Will looked through a crack in the brush. He was crouched down—waiting, hoping. He saw the rabbit fall. The big man walked within two feet of him. Will held his breath.

"All right, boy. Have it your way. But if you go for the cops, I'll kill her personally."

The man turned and walked away.

Will didn't dare come out for fear Scarface might hear something and come back.

He waited there, hardly breathing for what seemed an eternity. His mind was blank except for one thought . . .

Sarah.

CHAPTER 4

The first edges of darkness came. Will had moved to the shelter of the trees. He sat clutching his knees, thinking.

Sarah's mother and his grandfather would be worried by now. They had probably already called the sheriff. The only problem was, no one would know where to look for them.

What was the smart thing to do? Maybe he should go for help while he had the chance. After all, the police were trained to deal with this sort of thing.

No. That goon said if he did, they would

kill Sarah. Where did that leave him? Alone, that's where. He had to try to save her by himself. But how? It was one thing to pretend he was an Apache warrior, but it was another to actually pull it off.

Even with all the things his grandfather had taught him about survival, he knew he would have a tough time.

And time was short. The crooks could decide to leave at any minute. They could just shove Sarah into the pit and take off. Whatever he was going to do he'd have to do it soon.

He rummaged through his backpack. Ropes, flares, candles, a bottle of drinking water, apples, matches, and a small lantern.

Will bit his lower lip and thought. He remembered something his grandfather had told him and slowly he began to form a plan.

He grabbed the bottle, poured out the water, and filled it with lantern oil. Next he untied the bandanna from around his leg and stuffed it in the bottle, saturating it with oil, leaving one end sticking out like a fuse. He filled one pocket with pebbles and put his matches and flashlight in the other.

Quickly he lit the two flares and fired them into the sky, watching them arc red against the dark, knowing that by the time help arrived—if it arrived—his plan would have worked or failed miserably. Either way the police would be needed to clean up the mess.

Will repacked his backpack, slung it over one shoulder, and started toward the cave.

There was hardly any light, and he had to pick his way carefully. His leg throbbed, but he tried hard not to notice.

He watched the front of the cave for several minutes. It seemed odd that there was no guard. Obviously the goons didn't think of him as a threat. And as Sarah said, they probably knew a secret way out of the cave.

Will crept closer to the entrance. There was no noise. The first room of the cave was dark. He wanted to turn on his flashlight but knew he couldn't. He'd just have to feel his way.

The wall was slimy with bat guano. He made a face but kept going until he reached the first passage. That's when he heard the voices.

"Get the girl's pack and put some of the money in it. I'll put the rest in this bag."

Will moved down the passage toward the voices. He looked out from behind a large stalagmite. The two men were taking the money from the old trunk and stuffing it in bags.

At first he couldn't find Sarah. Then he spotted her. She was sitting on the floor near the side of the small cave. When she raised her head, Will drew a sharp breath.

One side of her face was a mass of purple bruises, and both eyes were black.

Will's eyes narrowed. They'll pay, he thought. Reaching in his pocket, he drew out some of the pebbles. He waited until he was sure the men weren't looking and then threw one.

It hit Sarah. She grabbed her shoulder and looked in his direction. Slowly she began to inch toward the opening.

Will took out his bottle and slid the matches out of his pocket. He had intended for Sarah to keep coming until she was out of danger, but the short man turned and caught her.

"What do you think you're doing? Get back over—"

Will lit the bandanna. He stood up and threw it at the short man's feet. It exploded into a ball of flame, setting the man's clothes on fire. Shorty screamed and rolled on the floor.

Sarah jumped to her feet and ran to Will. He grabbed her hand and bolted.

Scarface was right behind them.

Will veered to the left and ducked into one of the passages leading away from the palace room. Sarah stumbled and fell. Will pulled her up. They could hear the big man closing in on them. Will took another left turn and then another. Scarface's footsteps echoed in their ears.

Chapter 5

Sarah's heart was pounding. She leaned against the wall of the dark passageway and whispered, "Do you think we've lost him?"

"For now." Will sat down. "Are you okay?"

"Fine."

Will struck a match and looked at her face. She turned away. "They weren't too happy about my helping you escape."

He reached in his backpack and handed her an apple. "Hungry?"

"Starved." Sarah took a bite and spoke with her mouth full. "What do we do now?"

"Keep moving. I think I burned the short guy pretty bad. He won't be going anywhere for a while. All we have to do is stay out of Scarface's reach until the sheriff gets here."

"The sheriff?"

"I sent up both of those flares. Somebody's bound to see them and come looking."

Sarah was silent except for the noise she made chewing her apple.

"I know what you're thinking. You're wondering what will happen if they don't come. Don't worry, they'll be here. By now your mom has called out the National Guard. They're probably just waiting for a signal."

"I hope you're right."

"I am right. Want another apple?"

Sarah shook her head. "No, we'd better save them in case—you know, in case help is slow in coming."

"What's the story on these guys? Did you find out anything?"

"Not much. They're the ones who robbed the armored truck. Scarface was bragging that they got away with close to a million dollars. They were planning on staying up here until things cooled down and then taking off for Mexico."

Will stood up. "And then we came along and messed things up for them." He listened in the darkness. "I don't hear anything. Scarface must have made a wrong turn back there."

Sarah wiped her hands on her jeans. "I hope he fell into that bottomless pit."

"Speaking of that, from here on we're going to have to be more careful where we step or we'll be the ones at the bottom of the pit."

"Whatever you say. You're the captain of this expedition." Sarah stood. "Where to now?"

"I'd really like to find that other entrance. So far we've taken a left at every passage. I figure if we keep it up, it'll be easier to find our way back—if we have to."

Will turned on his flashlight to get a look at the passage they were in. It looked like all the rest. He quickly turned the light off. "Come on. Stay next to the wall, and take it easy."

They stepped out into the darkness.

CHAPTER 6

It was another dead end. They had hit several during the hours they had been walking and had to turn back each time. Will flashed his light around the room. "This is as good a place as any to stop. We'll rest here for a while."

"Will, have you been paying attention to the number of times we had to go one passage farther than the first left?"

"I've been trying to. Why?"

"This place is really getting to me. I don't like the idea of spending the rest of my life down here."

Will sighed. "Relax, Sarah. Just lie down and go to sleep."

"Humor me and tell me how many times."

"Okay. Three. We've hit three dead ends."

"It's four, Will."

"I knew that. I was just checking to see if you were on your toes."

"What if we can't find our way out?"

"Don't be dumb, Sarah."

"We could die in here looking for the way out."

"We could also die from a bullet or from stepping in a bottomless hole. Right now all we need to worry about is staying as far away from those two crooks as possible."

"I guess you're right." Sarah reached around in the dark to clear a place to lie down. "Will?"

"Go to sleep, Sarah."

"Shine your light over here."

Will took his light out of his pocket and pointed it in her direction.

Sarah had her hand on a human skull. She gasped and quickly pulled it away. "Ugghh!"

"Gross. Looks like the last guy who spent

the night here stayed permanently." Will flashed his light around the room. "Where's the rest of his skeleton?"

Sarah stared transfixed at the skull. "It's him. It's Red Horse. We've solved the legend after all these years."

"It can't be him. The statue is supposed to be hidden with the head, remember?" Will aimed the light at the skull. The eyes seemed to glow at him. Slowly he reached down and picked it up. Something fell out.

A small golden man.

They both stared at it. Sarah gently held it in the palm of her hand. "So this is what all the fuss was about."

"It's not very big."

Sarah ran her finger over the statue. It was shaped like an Apache warrior with his hands raised in prayer. "It was probably all they had."

Will knelt beside her. "I can't wait to see Grandfather's face when we show him this. We'll never hear the end of the legend now."

Sarah smiled grimly. "You mean *if* we get to show him."

Will put his hand on her shoulder. "No. I mean *when.* Don't worry. One way or another we'll get out of here."

"That's what I'm afraid of—that one way or another business." Sarah shivered then laid down on the cold, hard ground and tried to sleep.

CHAPTER 7

 Sarah sat up and stretched. She looked around the dark cave. "I was hoping I'd wake up and all this would be a bad dream."

Will was pacing back and forth. She watched him for a few minutes. "What are you thinking about so hard?"

He stopped. "I was thinking that maybe you're right. Maybe we have gone too far back. Chances are the goons are long gone by now. Why would they wait around? For all we know they left last night and we're hiding back here for nothing."

Will handed Sarah an apple. "What do you think?"

"We could check it out. If they're still here, we can always come back."

"True." Will zipped his pack. He flashed his light on for a second. "Let's go."

Sarah held her apple in one hand and the back of Will's shirt in the other. Will moved slowly, feeling each step before he took it. Four times he turned at the second passage, this time to his right, hoping to make up for all the dead ends they had run into earlier.

Will flashed his light around the walls of the fourth passage. Nothing looked familiar. He listened hard. Nothing. There was an eerie silence in the cavern.

"It doesn't make sense, Sarah. By now we should be close to the front of the cave."

"Face it, Will. We're lost. The best we can do is to keep wandering around, hoping to find a way out."

Will tried to backtrack in his mind. Where had he gone wrong? "Come on, Sarah. Somewhere between here and Red Horse's cavern we missed a passage."

Sarah fingered the statue in her pocket. "Maybe we shouldn't have taken it."

"What?"

"The statue. Maybe we should have left it for Red Horse."

"Sarah, I think this damp air is affecting your brain."

"It just doesn't seem fair. He's been looking for it all these years, and we find it by accident."

"Maybe we'll run into him and you can just hand it over."

"Will?"

"Yeah."

"Are you scared?"

"Would you believe me if I said I wasn't?"

"No."

"I'm scared, Sarah. Bad. But it doesn't do either of us any good to think about it." Will turned into the next passage. He flicked his light on. "Finally I recognize something. Remember that green pool, Sarah?"

She nodded. "I remember it but I couldn't tell you from where. How far do you think we are from the front now?"

Will turned the light off and scratched his

head. "It's hard to say because we were moving so fast. But it couldn't be more than four or five turns. From here on I'd better not use the light. Talk only if it's an emergency."

Sarah grabbed the back of his shirt again.

He took a couple of steps. "I've got an idea." He slipped his belt off and handed one end to her. "Hang on to this. It'll give us both more room to move."

They continued silently down the passageway, feeling along the wall for the next turn. Will stepped with his right foot. Suddenly there was nothing under him. The ground had disappeared. He lost his balance and fell forward, tottering on the edge of a bottomless hole.

Rocks around the rim of the pit began to crumble and break loose. As Will tumbled, Sarah fell with him. Her jeans ripped, and her knees were bleeding. The belt began to slip through her fingers. Sarah grabbed the belt with both hands and held on, keeping Will from falling over the edge. He dropped to the ground beside her shaking. "I—I thought it was the end."

Sarah held on to him. His breathing was short and ragged, and he fought to even it out.

"It's the statue, Will. Look at everything that's happened to us since we found it. Red Horse doesn't want us to have it."

"No. He's helping us, Sarah. I could have died just now but I didn't. Don't you see? Red Horse is trying to win back his honor."

Chapter 8

"Here's some medicine for that burn. I stole it from a farmhouse down the canyon. The people were gone. They'll never miss it."

The short man raised himself up onto one elbow. "If I ever get a hold of those two kids, I'm gonna skin them alive. The boy first."

Will pulled Sarah down behind a massive stalagmite. He held his fingers to his lips.

"He really did a number on your legs. You'll be lucky if you can still walk."

"I can walk. And I'll catch that kid if it's the

last thing I ever do." Shorty put some salve on his badly burned legs. "Did you check the back entrance?"

"I came in that way. Those kids haven't found it. Nothing's been disturbed. They're still in here somewhere."

"Good. Keep checking. There are only two ways out of here." He patted his gun. "I hope they choose to come this way."

Scarface sat on a boulder. "Why don't we take the money and run? Those kids aren't worth fooling with."

Shorty gave him an angry look. "Because I said we stay. I'm not gonna let some runts mess this up for us. If we move now we'll miss our Mexico connection. No. We'll sit tight. And in the meantime, we'll catch those kids."

Will jerked on the belt. Sarah followed him away from the palace room into a dark side passage. He leaned close and whispered, "We have to find that other entrance. When Scarface goes to check it, I'll follow him."

"What about me?"

"We won't make as much noise if only one of us goes. As soon as I find it, I'll come back for you."

"I don't know, Will. Why don't you stay here? I can follow him just as well as you can."

"Because I'm the captain, remember? Don't worry. They won't think to look for you in here. It's too close. Just stay out of sight until I get back."

Sarah was about to argue when they heard footsteps. Will moved to the front of the passage and pressed against the wall. He saw a light. Scarface passed right in front of him.

Will waited until the man was far enough ahead. Then he stepped out into the darkness and followed the sound of the footsteps, all the while trying to form a map of the trail in his head.

Scarface stopped suddenly. He turned and flashed the light behind him. Will froze. The light traveled up and down the shiny walls. When Scarface was satisfied that no one was there, he moved on.

Will let his breath out and started moving.

So far the path to the second entrance had been easy to follow. It was almost straight with only one turn at the second passage.

The big man stopped walking. He had reached what appeared to be a dead end. He pointed his light at the center of the room. Two ropes dangled from the ceiling. Scarface aimed the light at the top of the ropes.

A door.

There was a wooden door in the ceiling. Will smiled to himself. He couldn't wait to get back and tell Sarah. They were almost home.

Will had hidden himself behind a large boulder. He watched as Scarface checked the floor for tracks. The man made one last sweep of the room and started back.

This time Will waited until he could barely hear the man walking before he came out of hiding. He had the map in his head, and he didn't need to listen for the footsteps. All he had to do now was find Sarah and get out of here.

Cautiously he felt his way along, not putting any weight on his feet until he was sure there was ground underneath. His sneakers were noiseless as he walked.

Only a few more yards to go.

In front of him he heard an excited voice. A man was yelling. "I've got one of them."

Chapter 9

Sarah was restless. She moved closer to the front of the cave to listen. There wasn't much to hear. Occasionally the short man groaned and cursed, but that was all.

She could hear footsteps. That must mean Scarface was on his way back. And Will wouldn't be far behind. Silently she moved back into the passage. As she walked, something fell out of her pocket and clanked noisily on the stony ground.

It was the statue. She stood as still as possible, hoping that no one had heard it.

The footsteps came right up to her cave and stopped. Scarface pointed the light at her and smirked. "Well, well. Missed me so much you just couldn't stay away."

She tried to run, but he was faster. He dragged her into the palace room, where Shorty was resting, and threw her in a heap at his feet.

"Brought you a little present."

Shorty swung his legs around and stood over her. "Where's the boy?"

Sarah's voice was trembling. "We got separated. I don't know where he is."

"She's lying. You can bet he's around somewhere close. Go find him."

Will stepped back into the darkness. His mind was racing. How could this have happened? What should he do? He no longer had the ingredients for a homemade bomb. In fact, he had precious little left in his pack at all. A couple of apples, candles, and rope.

Rope.

Quietly he eased his way back up through the jet black passageway to the cavern where he had nearly fallen into the pit earlier. He took one of the ropes out of his pack and tied one end securely around a boulder.

He flashed his light to see what he was doing and then loosely wrapped the other end around the top of a jagged stalagmite.

Will took a deep breath and headed back the way he had come. The sound of Scarface's footsteps was coming closer. He swallowed hard and jumped out into the middle of the path.

Scarface raised his gun and fired. The bullet ricocheted off the walls. Rock chips flew as it hit again and again.

Will quickly moved into the next passage. He ducked behind an outcropping of rocks. Silently he picked up one of the rocks and waited.

The big man flashed his light around the room. His gun was poised, ready. "I know you're in here, boy. Don't worry. I'm not gonna kill you. At least not right now. The boss wants to have a little talk with you first."

Will stood up and aimed his rock at the man's flashlight. He let it fly. It hit its mark.

The light fell from Scarface's hand and shattered on the ground.

"I guess you think you're smart, don't you, kid? Well, you're not. This just makes things more interesting."

Will knew better than to answer. He slid out of his hiding place and headed for the next passage. When he was far enough in front, he spoke out. "You'll never catch me. You're too dumb—and ugly."

Scarface immediately moved in the direction of the voice. He was not accustomed to the darkness the way Will was, and he stumbled several times. Will heard him curse and smiled.

Always staying just far enough ahead that he was sure a stray bullet wouldn't hit him, Will kept making noise, leading his enemy on.

Scarface kept coming.

When he reached the cavern where he had left his rope, Will positioned himself to the side of the stalagmite. He picked up the end of the rope and held it loosely in his hands.

Will yelled, "Why don't you pick on somebody your own size, you stupid ape?"

Scarface stumbled into the room. Will

reached in his pocket and grabbed a handful of pebbles. He threw them at the sound of the footsteps.

"You think a bunch of little rocks are going to hurt me, boy?" The man snorted a tight laugh. "You're in over your head this time, kid."

Keep coming, Will thought. Don't stop now.

Scarface hesitated. "Where are you, boy? It's no good hiding. I'll find you sooner or later."

Will reached for the last of his pebbles. He threw them at the other side of the pit.

"Ah, over there . . ." Scarface took another step. Will jerked hard on the rope.

Scarface tripped and fell into the bottomless pit.

Will let go of the rope. He sat down to rest near the edge of the hole and wiped the perspiration off his forehead. He should feel bad. He had just killed a man. But he didn't feel anything. Just tired. And now he had to—

Out of nowhere a hand grabbed his shoe. A scream started in Will's throat.

"Help me, boy. If you don't, I'll take you down with me."

Will could feel himself slipping. Wildly he grabbed for the rope. His hand caught the very end of it.

The man had a good hold on his foot now. Will kicked violently. His body was sliding across the glassy floor toward the hole.

Suddenly his foot slipped out of his shoe. There was an agonizing yell that seemed to last forever.

Then silence.

Will grabbed the rope and worked his way up away from the hole.

Chapter 10

 "He should have been back by now." Shorty limped to the opening and pointed his light down the passageway.

Sarah edged toward the back of the room.

"No you don't. Not this time." Shorty pointed the gun at her and motioned for her to come closer. He grabbed her arm and squeezed. "From now on you stay right beside me. Understand?"

Sarah nodded.

Shorty pushed his hat back. "He must have

run into trouble." He looked down at her. "That boyfriend of yours is pretty sharp. You don't suppose he got the best of my partner, do you?"

Sarah forced a smile. "Actually he's kind of a genius. And he's been trained in guerrilla warfare by the old ones."

"Indians?"

She nodded again. "He's half Apache."

"If that's the case, maybe you and I better go have a look. You stay right in front of me, and don't try anything unless you want a bullet in your back."

Shorty shoved Sarah out in front of him and flashed the light up and down, searching each hollow and every possible hiding place. He called for his partner, but there was no answer.

He shone his light carefully around the walls of each passage they came to. Every few steps he stopped and listened.

"Something's wrong or he would have answered me by now. I'm not hanging around here anymore. This place is starting to give me the creeps."

He pushed Sarah back the way they had come. "We'll take as much of the cash as we can carry, steal a car, and go south."

When they reached the chamber where the money was stashed, he shoved one of the sacks at her. "Here. You're a big girl; you should be able to carry this."

Shorty grabbed a sack for himself and headed for the opening. "Come on, sister. Mexico is waiting."

A ghostly noise floated through the air. Sarah jumped. Had Red Horse finally come to rescue her?

The low whisper groaned again. As Shorty looked away from her, Sarah spun around and knocked the gun out of his hand with the money sack. Then she kicked him as hard as she could on his burned leg.

"Over here!" Will yelled.

She raced to the sound of his voice. He grabbed her hand and started running. "I know the way out. It's not far."

Sarah didn't talk. She just ran. Will led her to the room where the ropes were hanging from the ceiling. He hauled himself up and then reached down to help her. "Hurry, Sarah. Climb."

Will pushed open the wooden door. Sunlight flooded in. He scrambled out and pulled Sarah up.

They could hear angry yelling behind them. Will shut the door and looked around for something to put on it. The best they could do was a nearby hollow log. It wasn't very heavy but it might hold the door shut for a while.

"I thought you were Red Horse," Sarah heaved.

"I thought you were dead," Will said.

They flew down the mountain toward home. Sarah was in the lead. She looked back to see if they were being followed.

Then she turned and ran smack into the chest of a deputy.

CHAPTER 11

Grandfather was hanging on every word. "Then what happened?"

Will continued, "The sheriff had seen the flares and already had his men scouting the area. We showed the deputies the entrance to the cave. They almost had Shorty right there, but he slid down the rope and got away. They caught him trying to escape with the money on the other end."

"I'm so proud of you two."

"I just wish I could have brought the statue back for you to see," Sarah said.

Grandfather shook his head in amazement.

"I can't believe you actually had your hands on the statue."

"I really did." Sarah looked at the floor. "Too bad I dropped it."

"No. It's better that you left it in the cavern. That's where it belongs."

There was a knock on the front door. Will jumped up to answer it. He came back in the living room with a tall man in a black suit.

The man stood in the doorway. "As I told this young man, I'm looking for William Tucker and Sarah Thompson."

"That's us." Will pointed at himself and Sarah.

"I'm from the Dupont Armored Truck Company. The sheriff told me how to find you. My company has offered a reward for the return of our money and the capture of the criminals."

He went on, "I have the check with me. It's made out to both of you for the sum of one thousand dollars. All I need are your signatures." He flipped open his briefcase and handed them some papers.

Will and Sarah stared at each other. They

quickly signed the documents, and the man handed them an envelope.

He stood up to go. "By the way, do either of you know where I can find the gentleman who helped the deputies in the cave?"

"What man?" Will asked.

The agent raised one eyebrow. "I thought you knew. Apparently there was someone dressed in an ancient Indian costume blocking the criminal's escape from the main entrance of the cave. The sheriff tried to get an accurate description from the robber, but he refuses to talk about it. Oh, well." The agent snapped his briefcase shut. "Since you don't know him, I'll ask around town."

The kids watched him leave with their mouths hanging open. Could the agent have been talking about Red Horse?

Will was the first to come to his senses. "It's impossible. Isn't it, Grandfather?"

A mysterious look came over the elderly man's face. "Our people say that when you look at things with the eye, it might be impossible. But when you look with the heart, all things are possible."

GARY PAULSEN
ADVENTURE GUIDE

SPELUNKING

The adventure of exploring caves is called spelunking. Experienced spelunkers never enter a cave alone. A party of three is the minimum, and they always leave word as to where they're going.

From the moment you enter a cave make mental notes of landmarks. Whenever you turn off from the passage you are following, be sure to make some kind of arrow mark back to the exit that will not permanently deface the cave.

If you find yourself lost, sit down and keep calm. Reconstruct the route in your mind. See if you can locate your own tracks. Be systematic; explore one opening at a time.

If a passage doesn't seem familiar, mark it so that you won't try it again, and move on to the next one.

Should these clues fail, *do not panic*. Stay where you are, avoid wearing yourself out, and wait for the search party.

IMPORTANT EQUIPMENT

When spelunking, always bring
the following with you:

Flashlight or Lantern
Rope
Matches
Candles
Drinking water
Light food

Don't miss the exciting action coming soon!

GARY PAULSEN
WORLD OF ADVENTURE

Rodomonte's Revenge

Friends Brett Wilder and Tom Houston are video game whizzes. So when a new virtual reality arcade called Rodomonte's Revenge opens near their home, they make sure that they are its first customers. The game is awesome. There are flaming fire rivers to jump, beastly buzz-bugs to fight, and ugly tunnel spiders to escape. If they're good enough they'll face Rodomonte, an evil giant waiting to do battle within his hidden castle.

But soon after they play the game, strange things start happening to Brett and Tom. The computer is taking over their minds. Now everything that happens in the game is happening in real life. A buzz-bug could gnaw off their ear. Rodomonte could smash them to bits. Brett and Tom have no choice but to play Rodomonte's Revenge again. This time they'll be playing for their lives.

Escape from Fire Mountain

". . . please anybody . . . fire . . . need help."

That's the urgent cry thirteen-year-old Nikki Roberts hears over the CB radio the weekend she's left alone in her family's hunting lodge. The message also says that the sender is trapped near a bend in the river. Nikki knows it's dangerous, but she has to try to help. She paddles her canoe downriver, coming closer to the thick black smoke of the forest fire with each stroke. When she reaches the bend, Nikki climbs on shore. There, covered with soot and huddled on a rock ledge, sit two small children.

Nikki struggles to get the children to safety. Flames roar around them. Trees splinter to the ground. But as Nikki tries to escape the fire, she doesn't know that two poachers are also hot on her trail. They fear that she and the children have seen too much of their illegal operation—and they'll do anything to keep the kids from making it back to the lodge alive.

The Rock Jockeys

Devil's Wall.

Rick Williams and his friends J.D. and Spud—the Rock Jockeys—are attempting to become the first and youngest climbers to ascend the north face of their area's most treacherous mountain. They're also out to discover if a B-17 bomber rumored to have crashed into the mountain years ago is really there.

As the Rock Jockeys explore Devil's Wall, they stumble upon the plane's battered shell. Inside, they find items that seem to have belonged to the crew, including a diary written by the pilot. Spud later falls into a deep hole and finds something even more frightening: a human skull and bones. To find out where they might have come from, the boys read the pilot's story in the diary. Could he have eaten a crewmate to survive? And if Devil's Wall could force a trained pilot to do *that,* what dangers might the mountain hold for the Rock Jockeys?

Hook 'em, Snotty

Bobbie Walker loves working on her grandfather's ranch. She hates the fact that her cousin Alex is coming up from Los Angeles to visit and will probably ruin her summer. Alex can barely ride a horse and doesn't know the first thing about roping. There is no way Alex can survive a ride into the flats to round up wild cattle. But Bobbie is going to have to let her tag along anyway.

Out in the flats the weather turns bad. Even worse, Bobbie knows that she'll have to watch out for the Bledsoe boys, two mischievous brothers who are usually up to no good. When the boys rustle the girls' cattle, Bobbie and Alex team up to teach the Bledsoes a lesson. But with the wild bull Diablo on the loose, the fun and games may soon turn deadly serious.

Danger on Midnight River

Daniel Martin doesn't want to go to Camp Eagle Nest. He wants to spend the summer as he always does: with his Uncle Smitty in the Rocky Mountains. Daniel is a slow learner, but most other kids call him retarded. Daniel knows that at camp, things are only going to get worse. His nightmare comes true when he and three bullies must ride the camp van together.

On the trip to camp Daniel is the butt of the bullies' jokes. He ignores them and concentrates on the roads outside. He thinks they may be lost. As the van crosses a wooden bridge, the planks suddenly give way. The van plunges into the raging river below. Daniel struggles to shore, but the driver and the other boys are nowhere to be found. It's freezing, and night is setting in. Daniel faces a difficult decision. He could save himself . . . or risk everything to try to rescue the others, too.

The Gorgon Slayer

Eleven-year-old Warren Trumbull has a strange job. He works for Prince Charming's Damsel in Distress Rescue Agency, saving people from hideous monsters, evil warlocks, and wicked witches. Then one day Warren gets the most dangerous assignment of all: He must exterminate a Gorgon.

Gorgons are horrible creatures. They have green scales, clawed fingers, and snakes for hair. They also have the power to turn people to stone. Warren doesn't want to be a stone statue for the rest of his life. He'll need all his courage and skill—and his secret plan—to become a true Gorgon slayer.

The Gorgon howls as Warren enters the dark basement to do battle. Warren lowers his eyes, raises his sword and shield, and leaps into action. But will his plan work?